D1503079

Separate Sisters

Separate Sisters

NANCY SPRINGER

HOLIDAY HOUSE / New York

Library of Congress Cataloging-in-Publication Data
Springer, Nancy.
Separate sisters / Nancy Springer.—1st ed.
p. cm.
Summary: Thirteen-year-old Donni is so upset over her parents' divorce that she gets
into increasingly serious trouble at school and does not recognize how much her older
sister is hurting as well.
ISBN 0-8234-1544-9 (hardcover)
[1. Sisters—Fiction. 2. Emotional problems—Fiction. 3. Divorce—Fiction. 4.
Schools—Fiction.] I. Title.
PZ7.S76846 Sg 2001
[Fic]—dc21
00-047280

To Brooke

Separate
Sisters

chapter one

So I had what I wanted. Living with Dad. Mom not on my case anymore.

I had to be happy, right?

So I was in art class painting an attack heart. I was supposed to be painting the three gourds and an eggplant Mrs. Antonio had arranged up front, but it was Valentine's Day and I know girls are supposed to love Valentine's Day, but I hate it, I hate holidays and birthdays and all mushy occasions, so I was painting an attack heart, a long, messy, bright red, spear-shaped heart flying through the air with its sharp point about to kill—something, it needed something to attack, so I quick painted somebody with lots of red hair, and with the red still dripping on the brush I dipped into the black and painted big black letters I LOVE YOU TO DEATH.

There was this really annoying girl with too many pink plastic hair clips in front of me, and there was still a lot of paint on my brush, so I painted a big black attack heart on her back, right on her itty bitty, skinny-mini top from some French shop at the mall. She squealed like a guinea pig, and it was washable paint, for God's sake, like they use any other kind in school? So Mrs. Antonio came running. When she got there I was slapping black paint all over my painting, like the black letters I LOVE YOU TO DEATH had rained down on it, because I had suddenly realized that the person with a lot of red hair was my sister, Trisha.

"What is going on?" Mrs. Antonio wanted to know, and to cooperate and demonstrate I reached out and put some more black paint on the annoying girl.

A little while later I was sitting in the office waiting to talk with the vice-principal when my sister, Trisha the Perfect, walked past.

She saw me, and her mouth formed a soft *O* shape, and she came in. "Donni, what happened?"

That's the nine thousandth thing I can't stand about my sister, she's such a pet. She can walk into the office and they act like she's faculty, like she belongs there. They don't even ask her for a pass.

"Go away," I said.

She didn't go away. She sat down beside me. She was wearing dark slacks, just like the ladies who worked in the office, and a heather green scrunchie, and a heather green sweater that belonged to Mom. She and Mom swapped clothes a lot. But Mom wouldn't have touched my clothes without rubber gloves. I was wearing my favorite old, ripped high-topped All Stars, my favorite old, ripped baggy jeans, and my favorite old, ripped Texaco shirt, and I sure didn't need any doodad to hold my hair back because I keep it cut short.

All that, and people still say me and Trisha look alike because we both have red hair, though Trisha helps hers along with hair coloring, which is what she insists on saying instead of hair dye, and perm. We both have the same sort of boxy faces with jaw angles and cheekbone angles and short noses and freckles and green eyes. And I guess we both have two arms and two legs. So we look alike, big deal.

Trisha is only ten months older than I am. People say we look like twins, not just sisters. I say we should have been twins separated at birth.

Trisha asked, "Are you in trouble again?"

"Nooooo, I'm helping out the administration by holding this chair down. Leave me alone."

Even though Trisha is only ten months older, she is in eighth grade in all honors classes. I am in sixth grade because I got held back in kindergarten for being immature. Since then that's kind of become my middle name. Donni Immature Ross. I only see Trisha in school now because she lives with Mom and I have moved in with Dad. Next year, assuming she doesn't fail, which is not likely as she is an advanced-placement gifted-class genius and gets straight A's except in phys ed, she will be in the high school and I will hardly see her at all.

Good. Great. I can't wait.

Trisha got a look like an orphan calf, which she does really good, her eyes huge and pathetic under her curly bangs. She said, "Donni, why don't you tell me things anymore?"

Now she was trying to make me feel bad, and okay, I admit I don't understand me, I kind of wanted to talk to her. But then a tornado of emotions lifted me right out of my chair. I landed on my feet and stamped my Chucks and screamed at her, "Get out of my FACE just leave me ALONE!"

"Young lady!" a secretary barked at me. Trisha got up and backed out the door, her face white and taut.

I sat down feeling like an eggbeater was working on me, like I was a cake mix. I hated her, she was so tame, tame, TAME.

"Donni." Mr. Billet poked his head out of his door, probably hoping he'd kept me waiting long enough to make me sweat.

I went in and sat in the vinyl chair. Mr. Billet's office was utterly boring. Tan fake-leather chair, tan fake-wood desk, tan fake-something shelves. The only picture on the walls was *Washington Crossing the Delaware*.

Mr. Billet's face wasn't boring. Kind of like Mr. Potato Head. It might have been fun to rearrange his large features. But he looked bored to see me in his boring office. I'd been there often enough to make him tired of me. "Do you have anything to say, Donni?"

I shrugged. "I was fooling around in art class."

"Is that all? Any reason?"

I shrugged again.

"I see." I didn't see how he could see anything, but he leaned back and put his fingers together like a tepee and stared at me. "Mrs. Antonio says you could be quite good in art if you would just focus on the assignments."

I felt the eggbeater going again. I hated his flabby mouth. He should keep his flabby mouth off my art. Could be, schmudbe, I *was* an artist, which was exactly why I wouldn't do Mrs. Antonio's assignments. She should keep away from my art, too. But he'd never understand that.

"I had a talk with your elementary school principal, Donni," Mr. Billet said. "She says you never used to be a troublemaker. Obviously something has changed. Would you tell me what it is?"

I shrugged some more.

Mr. Billet picked up a fat manila folder and fake-looked at the papers inside it. "You can't afford to fool around in art, Donni. You are failing art. You are failing math. You are just barely passing music, health, science, and social studies. You have a C minus in English. Your only strong grade at this point is in phys ed."

I don't know why teachers and principals and people like that always inform kids of these things like the kids don't already know them.

"And these discipline problems don't help any," Mr. Billet droned on. "Mrs. Antonio says you painted on a girl's blouse in art. Why did you do that?"

"I don't know."

"That is not appropriate, Donni. It shows very poor judgment."

Not appropriate? Poor judgment? Why couldn't he be honest and scream at me and say I was bad, rotten, nasty, and mean?

Mr. Billet talked at me for another ten minutes before he gave me detention and let me go.

Just detention, like the other times. It was kind of disappointing. Detention is nothing. Just another study hall. I was in detention so much, it was like ninth period.

But Trisha knew I was in some kind of trouble, so she would tell Mom, so Mom would call Dad, so they would talk about me even before Dad got the detention slip in the mail. Mom would probably call Dad tonight. They would talk. Which meant I served a useful purpose.

*   *   *

Dear Computer,

Hello there. This is Trisha, your owner, beginning a new project, a journal. According to my English text, Chekhov kept a journal, and so did Virginia Woolf and just about all of the great writers. I wonder whether they were trying to feel less lonely when they started their journals. The text says Dostoyevsky believed one must suffer to be a true artist. It would seem I am off to a good start. Computer, I am fourteen years old and I feel as if you are my only friend.

Such being the case, I suppose I had better give you a name. For some reason, I believe you are a female computer, and your name is Amelia, after Amelia Earhart.

So let me try this again: Hello, Amelia. This is Trisha, and I am going to keep a journal on you.

I suppose what prompts me to begin is that I very much need a friend right now. Usually, the fact that I am considered a brain does not bother me unduly. Granted, some of my classmates choose to dislike me because I am gifted, but most days I just deal with it. Fact: I am intelligent. Fact: I am studious. Fact: I will be somebody. I will win a scholarship to a good college and perhaps I will someday write something important. I like to exercise my mind, and I am not going to pretend to be stupid just to be popular, and I don't care if kids call me a nerd. That is, on most days I don't care.

But today was Valentine's Day. Naturally, no one gave me a valentine. And to make the day even worse, Donni got in trouble again today, and when I tried to help, she screamed at me. We used to be very close. When we were little, we were always together, playing and sharing secrets. Back then, we were best friends. But ever since Mom and Dad split, Donni acts as if she's divorced me. I can understand why she took sides, and I can understand why she hates Mom, but why does she have to hate me?

As I write this, I can hear Mom on the phone downstairs talking with Dad about Donni. All Donni has to do is get detention and Mom runs to the phone. Now, according to Donni, I'm the pet? I beg to differ. Nobody pays that kind of attention to me, least of all Mom and Dad. Just because I get good grades and I don't do weird things like painting on people's shirts, do they think I don't have any problems?

I went to see Mrs. Antonio after school to apologize for Donni, and she showed me what Donni was painting at the time when she got kicked out. It was a picture of me. Donni has an astounding talent: just a few quick lines or brushstrokes and she's caught a person or thing on paper like a butterfly pinned there, as if she captured a soul. That picture was cartoonish and sketchy but it was *me,* Amelia. Alongside me, Donni had sketched a large tilted heart, and over-head, words in black, I LOVE YOU TO DEATH, with black raindrops falling down from them. Or perhaps they were black tears. But I'm not sure.

Still, it was the closest thing to a valentine that I received today. Mrs. Antonio gave it to me to take home, and I've hidden it behind my dresser.

Mom is finally off the phone. I can hear her heading up here, so I'd better start my home-work. Bye, Amelia. Nice talking to you.

chapter two

I watched Dad while he was on the phone with Mom. I watched his face get quiet, which means he's kind of concerned, but he didn't say anything much. He never does. Dad is just a big, sweet, sleepy teddy bear.

He got done listening to Mom, hung up the phone, and looked at me as mellow as ever. "What's the story, Donni?"

"This girl was annoying me in art class."

"Oh." He nodded almost as if he approved, like I had stood up to a bully. "You get detention?"

"Yes."

He nodded. "Try to behave yourself a little bit," he suggested, and that was all, as if he figured the school had taken care of punishing me. He sat down with his ergonomics journal—he was a mechanical engineer for a place that made shovels and ice scrapers and things— and kept reading.

All of which goes to show why I wanted to live with Dad. Mom, now—Mom would have been telling me I was grounded, no television for a week, straighten up and change my attitude, she was going to throw away my baggy jeans and sneakers and flannel shirts, sloppy clothing sloppy mind, I had to learn to live in the real world, I'd never get anywhere if I didn't learn self-control, discipline, and good study habits, look at the mess my room was, go clean it up right away and don't come out until it was shining, wasn't I ashamed wasting my potential, stop slouching, pay attention, she was trying to help me.

Mom is what she calls assertive and I call bossy. She is what she calls well-organized and I call neurotic. She is also pretty, with dark hair, dark eyes, a pointed face, and I cannot believe I came out of her; did somebody switch babies in the hospital? But then there's Trisha, who looks just like me but is just as retentive as Mom, minus all the yelling. Naturally Mom likes Trisha the Perfect a whole lot better than she does me.

Dad didn't say another word to me till bedtime, when he said, "Sleep tight, Donni." But that's normal. We don't need a lot of talk. We're comfortable together.

In the morning I got up, looked at how gray it was outside in the middle of February, thought about detention, and decided to keep myself home from school.

This was easy. Dad had already left for work—he had a long commute. He didn't get home until three hours after I did in the afternoon. He would never know I stayed home unless I told him. Sometimes I did tell him, especially if I had a stuffy nose or a cough. He didn't keep track, so he was really surprised when midyear reports came out to find that I'd missed twenty-nine days so far.

I felt so good about deciding to stay home that I wanted to tell somebody. Stupid me, I picked up the phone and called my sister.

"Yo, Trish."

"Donni!" She sounded glad to hear from me. "What's up?"

"Won't see you in school today." I didn't usually see her much, anyway. Not even at lunch. We had different schedules. "I'm siiiiick."

"You are?" Now she sounded worried. Trish has no sense of humor. "What's the matter?"

"Nothing. I'm skipping out."

"Donni, you *can't*." Now she sounded upset. "You already missed, how many days?"

"I've decided I'm going for fifty."

"Donni, c'mon, be serious."

Now she was making me annoyed and spoiling my mood. Why couldn't she lighten up? This was supposed to be fun. "You're worse than Mom," I said, and hung up on her.

At least she wouldn't tattle to Mom. Probably not. She'd have to call Mom at work if she wanted to drag me to school. Mom used to work part-time as a med tech in a doctor's office, but since the divorce she'd gone full-time. She was already on her way.

Siiiiick, I was so siiiiick. I went back to bed and slept in till eleven.

Then I ate a bologna sandwich in front of the TV. Daytime TV is pretty bad. I got tired of it after an hour and went for my art supplies. The apartment is small and there's no place for me to set up my stuff; that's the only thing I don't like about living with Dad. Someday I want a real studio. Meanwhile all I've got is a lapboard. I got it and my pad of drawing paper and the Prismacolors Dad bought me for Christmas, real expensive colored pencils, and I sat and drew out of my head. After three sheets what I was sketching turned into kind of an Eden scene with a wild landscape and lots of animals, bears, deer, wild horses, eagles, and other birds. I sketched in a woman and a man on the mountainside in hiking clothes, then a couple of little kids.

The whole thing gave me such a good feeling I just kept going. I added wild geese, alpine lilies, a waterfall, wolves, a big-eared fox, ground squirrels, and rabbits. I figured the sun at a nice low angle and colored and shaded everything. It didn't take long because I work really fast, but it was good. I'd hide it behind my dresser with my other good pieces. Usually what I did with my art, when I was being serious about it, was either throw it out or hide it. I hardly ever showed anything to anybody. If I showed something to somebody and they made fun of it or criticized, it would have been like they had taken it away from me.

When my Eden picture was finished, I set it up and looked at it with my heart toasty warm until I realized what I had done.

The man and woman were Dad and Mom. The kids were Trisha and me.

I grabbed the picture and ripped it up and threw the pieces on the floor.

I couldn't stay in that apartment with the shreds of my family lying around. I found my jacket and my key and headed out the door.

Down the fire escape. The apartment was part of a big old house in town, one of those monster Victorian places with bay windows and balconies and turrets. The expensive front apartments got all that stuff. Dad and I had a cheap back apartment.

I went out to the alley and started walking.

It was cold out there. Usually when I skipped school, if I went out it was just to walk to the Kwik-Mart on the corner and buy a pack of Twinkies or something. It was fun the way the people behind the counter looked at me and didn't do anything. This time, though, I found myself walking along the main road past the fire hall and the Lutheran church and the bra factory and the cigar factory that made the whole town smell like cider apples. And past row houses and a Dairy Queen to where the sidewalks ended and stubbly fields began, and I kept walking.

Okay, so I was heading—not home. Going to visit, that was all. Going to see the house where I grew up, the house in the country, where Trisha and Mom lived. Going to see—Trisha?

Okay, fine, this would be fun. There was a raw feeling in the air, like the gray sky might spit out some snow, but I didn't care. I could hike the six miles before Trisha got home. I would be sitting on the steps, real cool, when she got off the school bus. All the kids would see me there. I smiled, thinking of it.

Something drove up behind me and slowed down. I looked over my shoulder at a high-rider pickup truck with two scruffy guys in the cab, dirty bandanas on their heads. "Hey, baby!" one of them yelled. "Want a ride?"

"No, thank you."

They laughed, yelled a really disgusting suggestion at me, and roared away. I kept walking, but I didn't feel so good anymore, out there in the middle of nothing but cornfields. The gray sky felt too big, and I was getting cold. It wasn't that cold before.

A couple more cars went past, then something drove up behind me and slowed down again. My heart started pounding. If it was the yahoos again, and if they didn't go away this time, what was I supposed to do?

I turned around, and my heart kept right on pounding. It was a cop car.

It stopped. Township police car, one officer. He put on the flashing red-and-blue lights, got out, and walked over to me. "You lost, son?" He had a flat round face like a plate with a nose, and he knew I wasn't lost. He figured I was hooking out of school, and he sounded kind and sarcastic at the same time.

"No," I said. "I'm fine."

He changed his opinion of my gender without blinking. "Aren't you supposed to be in school, Miss?"

"I'm sick. I'm going to visit my mother."

"What's your name, Miss?"

I told him. He made me get in the back of the car, behind the metal grille, while he called me in. Then he U-turned the car and headed back toward town with me. I sat there looking at the doors with no handles on the inside and all the dashboard stuff I didn't understand, while he ignored me.

He took me to school, parked his cruiser, and let me out—just in time. My chest was feeling tight from being in a place I couldn't get out of.

He escorted me in. No handcuffs or anything, he didn't even touch me, but my chest kept feeling tighter. School was another place I couldn't seem to get out of. And every classroom we passed, people were looking at me.

He took me to Mr. Billet, who came out into the hall-way to meet us. "Well, hello, Donni," Mr. Billet said.

"I'm sick," I said.

"Sorry to hear that, Donni. You get sick a lot, and nobody ever seems to phone it in. Do you always go out walking when you're sick?"

But I was sick. My chest hurt and I felt hot and cold and sweaty, and my stomach was flipping and I felt dizzy and there was a roaring, pounding, thumping noise inside my head, and I felt like I was going to faint. But instead of fainting I leaned over and puked right on Mr. Billet's black wing-tipped shoes.

*   *   *

Dear Amelia,

Do you like being named after Amelia Earhart? Would you like a different name? I know it's traumatic to be stuck with the wrong name. My full name is Celene Patricia Ross. "Celene" refers to an ancient deity of the moon. Donni's name is Celadon Pamela Ross, but she will just about kill to keep it secret, she hates it so much. "Celadon" is a kind of delicate, pale gray-green Chinese porcelain, and I can't think of anything that is much less like Donni. As for me, I am certainly not a goddess, nor have I ever mooned anyone. Neither Mom nor Dad will take responsibility for inflicting those names on us, but it's obvious that at one point they thought they were being poetic and clever, giving us similar names, like we were twins. But we're not twins. We're not the least bit alike.

Actually, when we were younger we were alike, and we didn't mind our names. But after my eleventh birthday, suddenly I couldn't stand being called Celene, and I started making everyone call me Trisha. Then, monkey see monkey do, Donni decided she didn't want to be called Celadon anymore, so she became Donni. Instead of being alike, our names became very different.

Then Donni wouldn't wear the clothes Mom bought her anymore. She wanted boots from Sunny Surplus and a poncho from the Grateful Dead store. Mom wouldn't buy them, said she'd be wanting a barbed-wire tattoo next, so Donni hiked to the Goodwill and bought her own clothing, I suppose one can call it clothing, for a few dollars. I think she did it to punish Mom, but when Mom did not cave in and get her what she wanted, she pretended to like her pre-owned rags. Donni can be incredibly stubborn.

She got escorted into school by a police officer today. I don't even want to talk about it. I don't know why she acts the way she does.

I do know she's angry at Mom for the divorce. She's wrong; Mom was not to blame. But Donni always blames Mom for everything, like Mom is the wicked witch of the world when really she's not; she's just intense. She cares about getting things done correctly.

The big problem for me is: because I *won't* blame Mom, Donni is angry at me, too. She hung up on me this morning.

Amelia . . . do you want a different name? Emmy? Listen, Emmy, can you help me? Somehow I don't think so. You can help me with trigonometric functions, but I don't think you can help me with Donni.

chapter three

Mr. Grubb had passed out maps of the British Isles and we were supposed to be filling them in, but I was fooling around, turning Great Britain into a profile of Mr. Grubb. It worked surprisingly well. Cornwall was his big craggy chin and the Bristol Channel was his open mouth and Wales was his flapping upper lip and his warty nose, and I put a fierce eye where I should have labeled "Cheshire," and Scotland was his toupee flying off in the wind blowing across the Irish Sea. It was a caricature, but it was him. It was a lot of fun. Once the kids around me caught on to what I was doing they couldn't stop looking and snickering, and then other kids wanted to know what was funny, and as I was turning Ireland into the wind god blowing Mr. Grubb's toupee off, he came to see what the noise was about.

So next thing I was sitting in the office waiting to be talked at by Mr. Billet again.

I didn't know why I kept doing this. It wasn't like I enjoyed it. There was chilly sweat running down my ribs under my shirt. I kind of wished Trisha would come by, but she didn't. And then I didn't know why I wished that and it made me mad at myself and my head went fuzzy, like there was radio static inside it.

"Donni." Mr. Billet sounded ticked off.

He didn't bother with the fake-friendly stuff. As soon as I sat down in his office he said, "What happened this time?"

"I didn't do anything." It was the first time I'd lied. What was making me lie? My thumping heart?

He didn't believe me. "You can't go on like this, young lady."

"I didn't do anything!"

He slapped his hand down on the desk and made me jump. "Don't give me that. Listen to me. You cannot continue with your inappropriate behavior, Celadon."

He used my real name to tell me he was serious. But all it did was make my heart turn to a hot, hard, swollen rock earthquaking in my chest. Blood jumped in my temples. The insides of my arms twitched.

Mr. Billet said, "We are going to figure out right now what is making you act this way. It's up to you. You tell me, Celadon."

Was he crazy? I couldn't talk. I felt worse than I did the day the cop brought me to school. My chest hurt even worse, I was wet all over with sweat, my head felt like a loud amusement park ride spinning and I was shaking, shivering all over like I was cold even though I was hot, I felt like my insides were nothing but a sloshing mess, I needed to faint and I couldn't, I needed to scream or cry or something and I couldn't.

"I understand your parents are recently divorced. Tell me about the divorce, Celadon."

The sloshing mess exploded. Blew up like a home-made bomb out of a chemistry set. Lifted me off my chair. I opened my mouth and instead of puking on Mr. Billet this time I—words came out, sick words that burned my throat. Loud sick words. I can't tell you what I said to him. It was bad. My face was hot and cold and wet and I was shaking and the words kept spilling out of my mouth.

He flushed and reared up from his chair. "You're suspended, young lady!"

Now I was crying.

"Sit down. I'll have my secretary call your father to come get you."

"No!" I shouted. I didn't want my father to have to leave work, drive an hour to get to the school, when I could just walk home like I did every day. I could have explained that, but I could not seem to stop yelling and crying. "No, you're not calling anybody, you—!" I called him a name I can't repeat. I swore at him, and then I ran out. Out of his office and out of the school.

It started to rain. Good. Fine.

The rain mixed with the rain on my face as I walked home to the empty apartment. I didn't hurry. I felt like getting all wet. Maybe Mr. Billet would send the platter-faced cop after me. Fine. Let him.

I felt shaky awful. I had said sick things I didn't know were in me. I had gone out of control. I had yelled like a psycho.

Yet as the rain cooled me off and I calmed down, I started to feel good.

In a secret way, good. I felt almost happy, because Mr. Billet would call Dad and Dad would have to call Mom.

*   *   *

Dear Emmy,

Donni got suspended from school today. A boy I barely know stopped me in the hall and told me my sister was suspended. Then, just to increase the unpleasantness, he told me some of the things she said that got her suspended. Apparently the entire first floor of the school heard her.

Naturally, this evening Mom went over to Dad's place to discuss Donni with him, leaving me here, alone, to do my homework like the perfect daughter I am. Which I did. I sat here trying to write about Jane Austen with Donni's choice of swear words running through my head.

Then, when Mom came back, she marched straight up here and sat on my bed with that straight-lipped look she gets when she has decided on a course of action. She talked very softly, the way she does when there are difficulties. She said Donni is showing signs of instability. She said reaction to the divorce has Donni doing badly in school, which only increases Donni's stress, sending her into a downward spiral and putting her in danger of setting a pattern of failure for herself. She said Donni is in serious trouble, not just in school but in her life, and we have to help her.

I want to scream, yet I know she's right, Emmy. I must stop feeling sorry for myself. Maybe Donni is acting like such a jerk because she's feeling even worse than I am.

Anyway, Mom's plan is as follows: She, Mom, will check with all of Donni's teachers to see what work she can make up and what extra-credit work she can be assigned. And then, guess who is going to help Donni do all this homework? That's right, Emmy. Nice girl Trisha will save the day. Every evening, either Donni will come here or I will go to Dad's apartment to tutor her. I suppose when she comes here Mom might help her some. But Mom has mostly forgotten algebra, and the geography of Africa has changed, and so on. Dad could help Donni with math and science, but he doesn't. Why? He just doesn't, that's all. Exerting himself is not Dad's style.

So Operation Save Donni is up to me. More work for intelligent, sensible, dependable, responsible big-sister Trisha.

Actually, I almost feel like I want to.

Anyway, at least it will be a way of getting together with Donni more.

*   *   *

It went about the way I'd thought it would except for the really silly, mushy daydream stuff. Nobody cried. At first Mom interrogated me while Dad just sat there. But when I told them it was Mr. Billet talking about the divorce that made me lose it, Dad got an achy look on his face and reached over and touched my hair. Not a pat on the head. He just touched the side of my hair with two fingertips like to tell me he loves me. Dad is wonderful. I don't get to see much of him during the week when he's gone from seven in the morning till six at night, but on weekends we have the best times. Friday nights I go somewhere with my friends because Daddy's tired, but Saturdays are for Daddy. In the morning we go to the grocery and we always get the same stuff, lots of macaroni and cheese and spaghetti because that's what I cook on weekdays. And he gets some boneless chicken breasts because on weekends *he* cooks. We go to Burger King for lunch. We go to junk shops or garage sales and look at stuff. Then when we get home, Daddy makes rice in the microwave and cuts the boneless chicken breasts into strips and cuts up vegetables and stir-fries everything in peanut oil with a little fresh garlic. It's so good. Then we go to a movie. Daddy always says, "Want to take in a movie?" and I say, "Sure," so we go to the Cinemax. Then Daddy says, "Which one?" and I say, "Whichever," so we walk into one. We always choose without talking about it. We stand around and one of us kind of walks and that's it. It's great that we don't argue. We don't have to talk, talk, talk about stuff. And it's great being in the movie with Daddy like he's my date, even though he would never put his arm around me or anything like that.

But anyway, he touched the side of my head.

So Mom started talking and talking about what to do. Mom considers herself a solver. She talked up this plan about how I was going to do better in school and make up a lot of work. I tried to explain to her that they don't let you make up work when you're suspended, that's part of the so-called punishment, but she said that was no reason I couldn't keep up with my reading, they couldn't make me unread stuff once I'd read it, and maybe the teachers would let me make up work I'd kind of skipped *before*, and so on. Dad sat with just a hint of a smile the way he does when Mom gets going on one of her plans, like he knows it's not going to work, but he's not going to say anything. Which doesn't matter, because I can take care of myself. When Mom pushes me too far I just talk as loud and fast as she does. I didn't start to do that until she got on the subject of my clothes. She said I ought to start wearing nicer things to give me a proper mind-set for school and education. I said I don't care, I like my clothes, I like the faded colors and the way I look in them, and I don't see what clothing has to do with my intelligence, of which it is not my fault if I don't have as much as certain perfect people. She said she wasn't talking intelligence, of which I had plenty if I would just use it, she was talking attitude. I said my attitude would be okay if people like Mr. Billet would just let me alone. She said I had to learn to get along with the Mr. Billets of the world, there are a lot of them out there, called "bosses." At that point Dad almost kind of sort of laughed, and Mom gave him a dirty look before she kept going.

Anyway, Mom set up a plan for Trisha to help me with my schoolwork. Dad rolled his eyes. He and I both knew how that would go. Mom asked me to promise to cooperate with Trisha, and I said sure like it was a joke. I didn't mean it.

But then when Mom asked me to promise I wouldn't blow up at Mr. Billet again, I said yes. And I meant it. I didn't like to remember the way it had felt when I yelled at him. Like turning inside out. Like an alien was living in me. My chest started to hurt just from thinking about it. I didn't want it to happen again.

chapter four

So right after supper somebody knocked at the door. I got up and opened it, and there stood Trisha on the fire escape with a book bag full of work for me and more books in her arms.

"Trish," Dad said, and I was letting her in, but he got up and came over and took some of the stuff from her and touched her on the cheek with his fingertips.

All of a sudden I was so mad I could have spit. Trish was such a goody-nose, everybody liked her better than me, and, anyway, I couldn't stand the way she dressed, like a mini-Mom, black slacks and a gray turtleneck and a black bow—I wanted to rip that bow out of her hair. I wanted to throw paint on her to give her some color besides black and gray.

So we sat down at the table and Dad went back to his chair and Trisha tried to show me what I was supposed to do, but since she was acting like a schoolteacher I acted just the way I do in school. I fooled around and drew doodles on every piece of paper she put in front of me and didn't listen. Dad sat in the next room reading his magazine, and Trisha kept her voice sweet and patient, like she was such a superior being. Why wouldn't she yell? If she yelled, Dad might have to come see what I was doing.

He got up, but he didn't come near us. He went into the bathroom.

"I know what you're trying to do," Trisha said in a whisper as soon as he closed the door.

My hand and my pencil stopped like they'd run into something and I looked at her. This wasn't her prissy teacher-voice.

"Huh?"

"I figured it out," she whispered. "I know what you're trying to do."

"I'm not trying to do anything."

"Yes, you are. You're trying to get Mom and Dad back together."

That was so stupid. "You're nuts."

"No, I'm not. Every time you get in trouble they have to talk. That's what you're trying to do. Maybe you don't know it, but you are."

"You're out of your tree!"

Dad flushed the john and came out of the bathroom, so she didn't say any more, but she reached across the table and tapped her finger on the piece of paper I was doodling on. I looked down and there was a picture of Mom and Dad standing close together, talking.

I could have screamed. I balled up the paper and threw it at her.

Dad saw that. "Donni," he said, "what's the problem?"

"Nothing."

He came in. "How's she doing, Trish?"

Trisha said, "She's doing fine."

I didn't know that Trisha the Perfect ever lied. I stared at her, and she looked back at me with dusky green eyes that begged me to understand something, but I didn't know what.

*   *   *

Dear Emmy,

Who was it that said life is nasty, brutish, and short? Was it Hobbes?

Tutoring Donni is nasty, brutish, and takes forever. It's a disaster. So much for being a rescuing hero.

I've never felt worse. I've never felt so shut out. I go to Dad's apartment and the door is locked. And then I have to wait while someone comes to let me in. Donni's at home with Dad, but I'm a visitor.

Then Donni won't listen when I explain things, or even look at me. She's such a twit. Why won't she use her brain?

As for Dad, he tries to make me feel welcome, but he doesn't know how, and I can't tell him, because he doesn't like to talk. I can't, for instance, ask him to unlock the door before I get there, because he would look hurt and turn away. He and Donni probably get along fine, because she never wants to talk about her feelings, but I would not, repeat, *not* want to live with Dad. Donni is insane to think that Mom is to blame; can't she see it was *Dad's* fault? Mom tried and tried to get through to him, but he stonewalled her. He locked her out.

Ouch, Emmy, I sound as immature as Donni, don't I?

They are not going to get back together, either. I wish Donni would realize that.

Donni is so obstinate that she'll never admit to it, but I know why she's always in trouble: She's trying to get them back together. I know I'm right. It came to me in a moment of insight similar to understanding relativity.

Relativity. Ha! Get it? Donni's a relative, and I understand her.

Okay, that was lame.

Another insight is, I understand why Donni has so many friends and I don't have any. In a nutshell: Donni is fun. She's playful, and she

jokes around and does outrageous things and—
and she's a total rebel. I even like the way she
dresses, thumbing her nose at Mom and everyone else. I wish she liked me half as much as I
like her.

I wish anyone liked me.

Perhaps I'm more like Dad than I had realized. Aloof. No fun. Even when I try to make a
joke, it's no good. I don't get any practice,
because I'm so serious all the time. Maybe I
should talk about some of this to someone
besides you, Emmy. But I can't. I simply cannot
let Mom know how unhappy I feel. It would
worry her, and she has more than enough problems. She thinks I'm mature and solid in
myself, she depends on me, and I mustn't let
her down. I cannot possibly tell her I'd like to
just give up. Emmy, the only one to whom I can
talk is you.

*　　*　　*

I promised faithfully that I wouldn't do it again but I did.

I did it the day my suspension was over. I never even
made it back to class, and I really wanted to go back, to
see my friends and have a life again. Staying home was
boring. But before I could go back to class I had to see
Mr. Billet and apologize to him for the things I'd said to

him. That was fair. I really had said some sick things to him. I don't like apologizing and the idea of apologizing to Mr. Billet made my stomach hurt, but I could see that it was fair and I needed to.

So during the three days I was home I had painted a picture for Mr. Billet to present as part of the apology. His boring office needed some pictures on the walls. I didn't admit to myself at first that I was going to give the picture to him; I just painted it. First I did a picture of him standing in the hallway with the platter-faced policeman while I barfed on his shoes. I didn't put in a lot of barf, just the gesture. It looked like I was bowing to him, actually. It was a good picture and I took a whole day doing it right, Prismacolors and Windsor Newtons on heavy watercolor paper, but I decided he probably wouldn't like it. It was good, but he wouldn't want to be reminded of barf all the time. So I kept that one and did a whole other multimedia rendition, this one of Mr. Billet giant-sized straddling the middle-school building and riding it like a horse. It was simpler, yet it took even longer because I had to imagine the folds of his business suit and the sunlight coming down in glory spokes through stormy clouds and the wind in the hair, what hair Mr. Billet had left, and stuff like that to make him look noble. I used a dramatic angle, looking up at him, and put his head in profile against the clouds, and I did a really good job. It was my best work so far.

I couldn't hide it behind my dresser. I'd been so awful I had to give it to him to show that there was one good thing about me.

It was the first time I'd ever done anything like that, I mean made art especially to give somebody as a gift, except maybe some drawings when I was three years old and didn't know better. But there's a first time for everything. It was the first time I'd been suspended.

So the morning I went back to school I carried *Mr. Billet on Schoolback* sandwiched flat between two pieces of cardboard in a grocery bag. I waited in the office. My heart was thumping and I was sweaty and all the rest of it.

"Donni. Come in, please." He sounded like he was dreading this as much as I had been.

"I'm sorry, Mr. Billet," I told him right away, as soon as he closed his door. "I shouldn't have said, you know."

"No need to go into detail."

"I really am sorry. I apologize."

"Um, good, Donni." He seemed kind of surprised. "I accept your apology."

"Look, I brought you something." Carefully I pulled my painting out of the bag and laid it on the desk in front of him.

He sat there with no expression at all on his face.

I explained, "You need some art in here. I mean, besides *Washington Crossing the Delaware*."

"I see. It's very nice." My chest started hurting worse because I could tell he didn't mean it. He didn't even say thank you. He stopped looking at the painting and looked at me. "But your time would have been better spent on some of the subjects you are failing, Celadon."

"You don't like it." Stupid thing to say. Anybody could tell he didn't like it.

"That's not the point. The point is, you shouldn't be drawing pictures when . . ."

When I was behind in civics, algebra, etc.—but I barely heard what he was saying. My heart was pumping so hard I could feel the blood pulsing in my neck and temples. My face felt hot, yet my hands and feet felt cold. There was a tidal wave thundering and surging inside my head. Mr. Billet kept talking, something about appropriate behavior, efficient use of time, would I be drawing if I was sitting on the deck of a sinking ship, that sort of thing. It didn't matter what he was saying. All I understood was that he was trying to take away my art. He was trying to take away my art. HE WAS TRYING TO TAKE AWAY MY ART.

"Why don't you just poke my eyes out!" I didn't realize at first that I was screaming at him, but I was. Just as loud as last time. Leaning on his desk and screaming into his face. "Why don't you cut my hands off!" I needed windows, his office was a square tan prison with the door closed, no windows, and suddenly I felt like I really could not breathe. Like there wasn't air, like I was drowning or underground or something, my chest would burst, I would die, and there were words and noises coming out of my mouth and some of them were swear words, but they made no sense even to me, and I had to get out of there.

He didn't exactly suspend me that time. I sort of suspended myself. Running out of school is automatic suspension. I ran out.

I ran out of his office and out of the school. I was getting good at this.

But as I went charging out the door, I ran straight into Trisha.

I mean I really ran into her. I almost knocked her over. I was panting and crying so hard I couldn't see right.

Trisha took some courses in the high school and she must have been coming back from there. I knocked her books and pencils all over the sidewalk. Her calculator broke open and the batteries rolled out.

She squeaked, "Hey!" like a mouse that's been stepped on. "Donni, for the . . ." But then her voice changed. "Donni, what's wrong?"

I was what I guess you would call hysterical. I couldn't talk.

Trisha said, "Calm down," and she put her arms around me. I leaned against her, but I still felt like I couldn't breathe. I kept gasping for breath. It was worse than cry-ing, worse than sobbing. Though I was crying, too.

"Shhhh," Trisha said, patting me. "Just relax. It'll be okay." She sounded like she almost believed that. "Tell me what happened."

I heard a bell ring, and I managed to choke out, "Go in. You'll be late."

"I can be late for once."

I stood back from her. "You—you'll get detention."

She didn't even move to pick up her stuff. "I can get detention for once."

She lifted her chin as she said it. And I knew she was scared to death of detention or ever doing anything bad. I mean, she'd never had detention in her life. She'd risk it for me?

All of a sudden I calmed down. "I'm okay now. You'd better go in."

"Not till you tell me what happened."

"Nothing happened except that I'm a certifiable lunatic and I've got suspension again." I gathered up her stuff for her and handed it to her. "I'm going home. See you tonight."

"You sure you're okay?"

"Yes."

After she was through the door and it was too late for her to hear me I added, "Thank you."

I walked home. I had lied when I said I was sure I was okay. Actually, I was starting to feel pretty sure there was something wrong with me, and it scared me. Even the idea of Mom and Dad getting together and talking with me didn't help, because I'd been thinking about what Trisha had said, that I was getting in trouble to try to get them back together. It made me so mad I knew it might be true. But if that was it, then it wasn't worth it. They were never going to get back together. They probably shouldn't get back together. All I was doing was hurting myself.

I would stop getting in trouble. I would just plain stop. It was that simple.

But I had meant to stop when I promised. And here I was again.

chapter five

Dear Emmy,

Please forget all that talk of understanding Donni. Evidently it was premature. And please forget anything negative I said about her, because now I am truly worried about her. Something is very wrong. When Donni ran out of school today, she was not just upset and she was not just being a jerk. She looked as though she was out of her mind with fear, her face so white that her lips looked blue. She was crying as though someone had beaten her or tried to kill her. I have never seen her look so terrified. She seemed so frightened that she frightened me, but I didn't show it, because someone needed to be strong. Inwardly, I was shaking, and I still am.

After she had calmed down somewhat, I went into the school, and Mr. Billet met me in the hall and demanded to know whether I'd seen Donni. When he found out I'd let her go home, he yelled at me. He said I should have made her come back in and talk with him. I've never been yelled at even by a teacher, let alone by Mr. Billet, so that was a first.

By the way, Emmy, I have detention. That is another first. But I suppose one who wants to be a writer should welcome new experiences.

Mom is so worried about Donni, Donni, Donni that she barely noticed when I told her I had detention. She doesn't even care.

I am noticing my own tone of voice and I sound brattish. This must stop. I need to grow up. Mom is right to worry about Donni. Now I know what it is to worry about Donni as well.

*   *   *

The school insisted on a big meeting with Mom *and* Dad and the school psychiatrist and the guidance counselor and the principal and Mr. Billet and me. Three women, three men, and me in pick-a-gender overalls with one shoulder strap hanging. Mom and Dad both had to take time off from work, but neither of them acted mad at me. That made me scared because it showed how serious things were. But what made me even more scared was what might happen. Not what anybody might do to me, not detention or suspension or anything, but I was scared of what *I* might do. What might go on inside me. The awful weirdness hurting my chest and burning in my throat. The shakes, the sick feeling, the awful words vomiting out of me. I was more scared of me than I was of anything. I was so scared of me that I was feeling shaky and my chest felt tight and my stomach felt queasy just from thinking about it. About not wanting to be that way.

I made up my mind not to say anything. Not a word. Not even if they yelled at me or thought I was sulking. If I didn't say anything, then I couldn't say anything sick, and I might get through the meeting.

So there we all were in the conference room behind the office, in cushy swivel chairs around a big table, like the board of directors. It was a little better than Mr. Billet's office. At least there were windows.

Mr. Billet started things off by filling us in on the history, as he called it. He was fair. He didn't make it sound any worse than it was. "Donni apologized with apparent sincerity," he said when he got to telling about the second time I had flipped out at him. "Then she immediately presented me with a painting—"

"She *did?*" my mother exclaimed. Mr. Billet just looked at her. Nobody was supposed to be interrupting, but my mother was so intent on what she was thinking that she kept right on going. "You must *rate,*" she said awed. "Donni never gives art to anybody."

At least somebody understood. I almost smiled at her. Go, Mom.

Mr. Billet looked at her like she had extra heads. "My impression is that Donni uses art as a crutch—"

Mom interrupted again. "What sort of picture did she give you?"

"I felt it was not very appropriate—"

"Do you still have it?" the school psychiatrist asked. She was a dyed blonde and needed to take care of her roots. "May we see?"

If he'd thrown it in the trash—no. No. I must not say anything. Must not think anything, either. Must not go weird again. Must not. Must not.

"It's not really—"

"I'd like to see also," said the guidance counselor, who was younger and skinnier and had a better dye job.

Mr. Billet mumbled something and went to his office. A minute later he came back with my painting. At least he hadn't ripped it up.

The room got stop-the-world silent as everybody looked. Usually there are small noises in a quiet room. People sniffing, tapping their fingers, moving their chairs. But there were no noises. None.

Then Mom turned her head. "Donni," she said straight to me, "that is *fantabulous.*"

"It's absolutely extraordinary," the principal said.

The guidance counselor was nodding and staring.

I breathed out.

"Huh," Mr. Billet said. "Well I, uh, I didn't feel it was the best use of her time. I don't know much about art."

The school psychiatrist sat up straight. "But aside from the exceptional talent that's displayed in that piece, don't you see what Donni was trying to *tell you*?"

"Uh, no." Mr. Billet looked hassled. "I, uh, I don't."

"Well." She took a breath to talk, then changed her mind and turned to me. "Donni. Perhaps you can explain it better than I can."

I shook my head and curled deeper into my chair.

"Donni, go ahead," Mom urged.

I couldn't if I wanted to. I was shaking.

Mr. Billet said, "None of this changes the fact that Donni then flew out of control and started to abuse me, using highly inappropriate language, very similar to the previous time."

"Donni," the principal asked, "do you have anything to say?"

I shook my head.

"We'd really like to help you. Can you explain your conduct to us? Tell us what is going wrong?"

I put my hands over my mouth.

The school psychiatrist was looking at me and she understood better than the rest of them, dark roots or no dark roots. "She looks very pale," she said. "Donni, do you need to be excused?"

I nodded and got out of there. I sat out front even though it was cold, because I felt better in the fresh air. I sat there till my parents came out nearly an hour later.

"Okay," Mom told me, "you go back to school tomorrow, on one condition."

"Apology?"

"No. Not this time. But you're supposed to see the psychiatrist."

My father smiled at me like it was all nonsense. He hadn't said a word.

This is the part I'm ashamed of. Most of the rest of it I don't mind telling about. It's like, I had some problems and made some mistakes; so does everybody. Dumb stuff happens. But this part—I really wish I could take back what I did.

So I was back in school, and Trisha was coming over every night to help me with my homework or at least make me do it, and I didn't like it, she acted like a teacher, so I acted like a kid who hated teachers, but it was sort of kind of working. I felt like school was going a little bit better. I was still getting detention for tardiness and lost books and dumb stuff like that, but I was staying out of Mr. Billet's office. So I began to think I might pass the year after all. There was this big English assignment, which counted a lot, and I had to type it, but Dad's computer was down. So the Sunday before the Monday it was due I had Dad drop me off at Mom's place so I could type it on Trisha's computer.

It was this analyze-a-poem paper. Rhyme, meter, imagery, symbolism, all that. There were some poems in the book I absolutely loved.

So it must have been after the birth of the simple light
In the first, spinning place, the spellbound horses walking
*   warm*
Out of the whinnying green stable
On to the fields of praise.

I love that. It makes me see the most amazing pictures in my head. But I couldn't write about something I loved. I couldn't let anybody know, least of all a teacher. Look what had happened when I gave Mr. Billet a painting. So I chose an Emily Dickinson poem because I think she was a creepy old hag.

Because I could not stop for Death,
He kindly stopped for me . . .

She sure didn't give me any pictures in my head, but it was easy to analyze the meter. This poem could be sung to the tune of "The Yellow Rose of Texas" and sounded better that way and I said so. I also said it used personification to convey abstractions and it tried to be important, but nothing seemed real. The horses drawing the carriage with their heads pointed toward eternity didn't seem like real horses. I said a lot of stuff. Trisha helped me. She was good at this.

"Why don't you type it up for me?" I invited her.

"Type it yourself, Donni." She sounded cranky. She went downstairs and sat in front of the TV set. She seemed tired.

I got halfway through typing my paper and I was ready for a break. But I didn't want to leave Trisha's room because if I went anywhere near Mom she would want to talk with me about school. So I started fooling with Trisha's computer. I don't like computers much, they're Trisha's thing, but I was bored, so I figured I'd try a computer game. But, duh, there weren't any. Like, this was Trisha's computer, and it had a calculator and a clock and a note-taking program and a calendar and schedule and all sorts of rinky-dink stuff but no cool screen savers and no games, either. It was annoying, like Trisha. I clicked on File Manager and browsed through the file titles, just fooling around, and I saw one called Journal and I clicked on it.

And I read it.

A lot of the time I just want to cry . . . Donni acts as if she's divorced me . . . I miss her . . . Maybe she'll stop hating me if I can help her . . . I wish she liked me half as much as I like her . . . I wish anybody liked me . . . Emmy, the only one I can talk to is you.

My big sister, Trisha, lonely? Talking to a computer? But—but no, that couldn't be. She was a liar. She was perfect. Everybody liked her better than me. She—missed me? I felt like I wanted to cry, I felt so bad, but at the same time the mix-it machine was cranking up inside my head, roaring in my ears, and the eggbeaters were going and my heart felt hot and the feeling that I wanted to go to her got spun away in the garbage, got all flipped around. Trisha had pain, Trisha had problems? But she was supposed to be the mature one.

NOBODY WAS ALLOWED TO HAVE WORSE PROBLEMS THAN I DID!

My sister, talking to a computer named Amelia. What a twit. I grabbed at the mouse, shaking, I was so angry. I stabbed at the button. Select *Journal*. Delete. Bye-bye Emmy.

I left my paper half finished and stomped downstairs. Mom and Trisha were sitting one at each end of the sofa in sweaters that practically matched, like bookends.

"I read your stupid journal," I said to Trisha real hard. "I read the junk you wrote about me."

Her mouth came open. Her eyes opened wide, frightened and hurt, like I'd shot her or something.

"I erased it," I said. "Don't write stuff about me." I walked out without my jacket and headed home on foot.

chapter six

Mom came after me, of course. I was moving fast, but she caught up to me in the car. She pulled alongside me when I was a hundred yards down the road, rolled down the passenger window, and ordered, "Get in."

There was a crisp edge to her voice. I got in.

"Trisha's crying," Mom said. "What's going on?"

"Nothing. Take me home."

"I will do nothing of the sort." She U-turned in a dramatic gravel-spraying way, and Mom is not the gravel-spraying sort. "You two work this out."

When we got back into the house Trisha was up in her room. We could hear her sobbing and moving around up there. "Go on," Mom told me.

I didn't want to. But even though I hadn't had time to think it over, I already knew I had done wrong. My head was trying to say hey, so I lost it for a minute, so what, it was just a stupid journal—but my gut knew

I had done something bad, I had to try to fix it. So I went up.

Her room door wasn't locked and I didn't knock, just walked in. Trisha's room is usually perfect like her, but now it was a mess, bits of mad litter all over the place. She had ripped up the handwritten draft of my English paper into pieces as small as confetti, and I just knew (and I was right) that she had zapped the file on the computer and she was ripping up my picture of her and the attack heart.

Right, she'd mentioned it to her precious Emmy. I had meant to find it and take it back or trash it. But it was one thing to rip it up myself and another thing to see her do it. She ripped the heart in half and it was like she was ripping me down the middle. I stood there like she'd hit me.

There were tears all over her face and dripping off her chin. Snot, too. Her eyes were red and glaring, her mouth twisted with crying. "Get out of here!" she screamed at me.

I stood stunned.

"Go away! I hate you!" She jumped me, and I was the one who got A's in phys ed, but boy was she strong. She shoved me out of the room, slammed the door, and locked it.

I went downstairs. "She tore up my paper," I said to Mom.

"She *what*?"

"She tore up the paper I was doing on the computer."

Mom started upstairs.

"Mom, don't." It was kind of nice to see Trisha the Perfect in trouble for once, but I hated myself for feeling that way.

"But she can't do that. You need to get that paper in."

To me the paper was the least important thing, but to Mom it was the most important thing. And I couldn't explain why Mom was wrong. I felt tired, tired, tired. I said, "Please just take me home."

She got a funny look on her face—like I wasn't home?—but she did it.

I couldn't sleep that night. I kept thinking about Trisha. About three in the morning I turned over and sighed and all of a sudden I understood why I should never have messed with her journal. I mean, I knew it was not nice and it was against the rules, like I ever worry about rules, but all of a sudden I really understood. In my heart. The thing was, I'd never thought about it much, but to Trisha writing was like art was to me. That journal meant so much to her she would never have shown it to anyone. Just like I'd never shown my best paintings to anyone up till I'd lost my mind and given one to Mr. Billet.

Besides, Emmy was her friend, and I'd killed her. I'd killed Trisha's only friend.

I wanted to hit me, but I was too tired. I just lay there.

*   *   *

61

The next morning I went to school with my head feeling like it was stuffed with Rice Krispies and the rest of me feeling like total slime. I walked around the school looking for Trisha and I found her in the lobby, but then I couldn't think what to say to her.

It didn't matter. I never got close to her. When she saw me standing there she glared, turned her back on me, and walked away.

My chest hurt, and my gut. I went to science, but I couldn't stand the way I felt. Trying to do something, anything, to lighten me up, I took the pickled earthworm I was supposed to be dissecting and stuffed it up my nose so most of it hung out. I took somebody else's earthworm for the other nostril. They stunk pretty bad, but it was worth it because kids were laughing and yelling, "Ewwww, gross!" Then I made smacking noises and pulled one of the earthworms out of my nose and held it dangling while I tipped my head up and opened my mouth to eat it.

The teacher yelled, "*Miss* Celadon Ross!" and that was all it took.

I went psycho. I threw the worms at her. I screamed, I swore. It felt like my chest was going to blow up. I couldn't breathe. I ran out of the room and out of the school.

I don't even want to talk about it, I was so sick of me. I hated me.

So there I was, suspended again, walking home from school and it wasn't even noontime yet, gee, what else was new? But I didn't make it all the way home. A car honked, and I looked, and it was the school psychiatrist, and she still hadn't gotten her roots bleached. Maybe she was letting her natural color grow out. Anyway, she pulled the car over to the curb and turned it off. Her mouth was set like a mousetrap and she beckoned me.

I got in the car with her. "What happened?" she asked. Teachers and administrators and people like that always ask what happened, and I don't see why they bother because usually they already know in one way and in another way they don't want to know.

I told her, "Nothing. I flipped out."

I'd been to her office for counseling four times and so far I'd done a really good job of not telling her anything. I mean, not anything true. I wanted to keep her happy, of course, so I told her interesting things, such as my mild-mannered father was really a mole for the CIA and he had met my mother through the Witness Protection Program and my mother's real identity was known only to the Mafia, she was a professional pyromaniac who could be hired to set people's hair on fire and see how they looked as human candles. Stuff like that. The last couple of visits I'd gotten the feeling the shrink was pissed at me and today I was sure of it.

She said, "Donni, this won't do."

"Do what?"

"Listen to me, youngster, would you please help me to help you? You don't seem to understand the consequences of your actions. One more escapade and you'll be expelled. You're only twelve—"

"Thirteen."

"You're only thirteen years old. The state can't allow you to go without an education. They'll take you and put you in a reform school."

Reform school?

"I am serious."

I could tell she was serious. My blood was freezing. And I felt the pressure building inside my head and neck and chest; I knew that feeling. If I stayed in that car with her one more second something awful was going to happen. The weird, wild stuff inside me would come flying out and I might strangle on it and die, I might say things, I might hurt her. I had already hurt Trisha.

I opened the door and ran like a rabbit.

Tires screeched and a car horn blared; I was so crazy I had run into the street. But I was on the other side now. Running home. Run. Run. Get help.

I ran panting and crying down the alley. Across two more streets, just barely dodging the cars. Through the weedy backyard, up the fire escape, into the apartment, and I phoned my dad at work.

"Dad? Dad! They—they say they're going to send me to a reform school."

"Donni?" His voice sounded laid back and mellow as always.

"Dad, help me. They're going to take me away."

"Donni, calm down. Where are you?"

"Home. I ran out again. They say if I do it one more time they're going to take me away!"

"So don't run out anymore."

"But—" But I didn't want to flip out and run, I hated it, but something made me keep doing it anyway.

"Just make up your mind," Daddy said like we were talking about groceries.

"But I—I need—"

"It's not a problem. I've got a meeting, Donni. See you tonight."

I was shaking so hard it took me three tries to get the phone hung up. I needed help. Run. Run. I couldn't stand still to think who else to phone. I ran out the door.

My legs and my pumping arms and my thumping heart knew where to go and had me halfway there, halfway to the other end of town, before my mind caught up with them. Trisha said I'm stubborn, okay, I am stubborn, but that's my head. My heart knew enough to point me toward the person who would help me.

Mom was in the hallway of the doctor's office where she works when I burst in like a wet cyclone. I was panting and gasping and crying so hard I couldn't talk even to call her name. Her eyes widened and she opened her arms to me and I lurched into her hug and bawled.

I'd been doing an awful lot of crying, but I guess I really needed Mom's shoulder to cry right. She held me and patted me and cuddled me and kissed my head and smoothed my hair and I cried and cried. When I finally came up for air and a Kleenex, I found that sometime when I wasn't noticing I'd moved from the hallway into the doctor's office. Mom was sitting in his big leather chair and I was sitting in her lap; she was holding me like a baby.

"Jeez," I muttered, getting up. I blew my nose and sat on the floor beside her and laid my head against her leg because my face felt hot. She stroked my hair.

"Okay? You going to tell me what's the matter?" Aside from the divorce, she meant. She already knew a lot of what was the matter. "Take your time." She was so sweet, so gentle, like Trisha—I had that backward; Trisha was like her.

My head felt like it was going to split wide open. "They say they're going to send me to reform school."

"*What*? Who says?"

"The shrink. She says if I run out one more time they'll take me away."

"Is that true? Can they really do that?" I realized she was talking to somebody else. I swiveled to look and there was the doctor standing in the doorway, checking on us. He could have been ticked off with me bawling in his office and taking Mom away from her work, but he didn't seem to mind. He had kind eyes.

"In this state, yes," he said. "They can."

"We won't let it happen, Donni," Mom told me. "I'll get you into a private school if I have to. Or I'll home school you."

I knew she absolutely meant it. But what if something went wrong, what if the law wouldn't agree to Mom's plans, what if—

She said, "Explain to me why you run out of school."

I couldn't. How could I tell anybody I had horrible stuff inside me? They'd know I was crazy. Forget reform school; they'd lock me up in a nuthouse.

Mom said, gentle as a feather, "C'mon, Donni. Give me a clue. What's making you act the way you do?"

"I—I don't know."

"Yes, you do. Truth, sweetie. What's going on?"

I shook my head.

"Honey, you can tell me."

Couldn't.

But—but this was Mom. . . .

I laid my head on her knee and told her. I told her about all the weird stuff, the noises in my head, the cold hands and hot face and feeling like I couldn't breathe, the shaking, the pain in my chest and stomach, the way filthy words spilled out of me and I couldn't hold them back and I felt totally nutsoid out of control, and I felt like I was going to hurt someone.

"There's something wrong with me." I was crying again, but I was too tired to cry hard.

"It's probably just stress." Mom was stroking my head, and I could tell by her voice that she was worried, but she was trying not to worry me. "Some kind of panic disorder, maybe. Anyway, it's something physical, maybe biochemical, so it can probably be treated, Donni. Doctor—" She was talking past me again, to her boss in the doorway. "Can we get her a referral? And a medical leave from school?"

"Absolutely."

"Donni, now just relax. We can handle this." Mom reached for the phone and called the school—she knew the number by heart. She asked for Mr. Billet. "Donni's very upset," she told him, and she explained why. Her voice was calm and precise. She wasn't yelling at him, but he could tell she meant business. They talked awhile. He told her his side. All the while she was smoothing my hair, stroking my neck, rubbing my back and shoulders with her free hand. In her calm, even voice she said to Mr. Billet, "You're treating it as a discipline problem, but it's not just a discipline problem. It's a health problem, a physical problem, and an emotional problem. I would appreciate it if you would add those dimensions to your thinking."

She told him she would bring a medical excuse to the office, and she wished him a very good day and said good-bye.

There was a sofa in the doctor's office. Mom asked me, "You want to lie down and rest while I take care of the paperwork?"

I nodded. "Mom," I said, shaky but talking fast because I wanted to get this over with, "I called Dad, but he didn't want to do anything."

She sighed. "That's the way your father is," she said. "He doesn't deal with things. He's not a problem solver. But he loves you very much."

chapter seven

So there I was home alone again. This was not making me happy anymore. I was getting really sick of being a sicko, and I wanted to be in school. I mean, I didn't like schoolwork, but I liked *school*. I wanted to be with the other kids.

This wasn't the same as being suspended. The doctors weren't sure yet whether I had depression with paranoia or panic attacks or post-traumatic stress or what, or whether they should give me medicine, and until somebody got a clue I was on what they called "homebound." Tutors would come see me. I would do my work and get my grades. All the work of school and none of the fun. I couldn't even call Trisha. She was in school.

She was mad at me.

She had a right to be mad at me.

She was so mad she might never forgive me.

I felt really bad.

I slept late, got up, yawned around, watched a little TV, lost track of time. When the doorbell rang I opened the door without looking out the peephole because I assumed it was Mom. She had said she was going to come see me over her lunch hour.

The person standing at the door was Mr. Billet.

At the sight of him my heart started to pound and my head started roaring and I started shaking. I took a step back, but I had to hang onto the doorknob because I felt like I was going to fall.

"My word," he said, looking anxious. "I can see what the medicos mean. Heavens, Donni." He lifted his hands like to show me he was not carrying a weapon. "I'm sorry. I wouldn't hurt anybody."

"It's okay," I managed to say. I was taking long, deep breaths the way the stress doctor's therapist had told me, and that was helping some. "I'm just surprised." Seeing him there when I wasn't expecting him had spooked me so much it had shown. Usually I would have been able to hide it.

"This is not an official call," he said.

"Oh. Uh, come in?"

"No, I'll just tell you what I want. I was wondering if I could commission some artwork from you. For my office. You're right, it needs something on the walls." He must have seen a funny look on my face because he started talking faster. "The piece you did for me, I'm going to get it matted and framed, but I'm going to hang it at home, not in the office. It seems too, how shall I say, egotistical for the office. I'm not the principal, so having me riding the school . . . well, I don't feel right. But you're extremely, extremely talented. Perhaps you could come up with another theme? Without me in it? George Washington is coming down. He gives me the heebie-jeebies."

Standing on my doorstep and talking fast like that he just seemed like the spot-remover salesman. All of a sudden I wasn't scared of him at all.

"Mr. Billet," I said, "would you like to see the picture I did of me barfing on your shoes?"

"*What?*"

"C'mon in." I beckoned him into the living room and went and got the picture and showed it to him. His jaw dropped. He gawked for a moment then burst out laughing. He threw his head back and laughed so hard I had to smile.

"That's amazing!" he said, chuckling. "Donni, you have an astounding knack for catching a likeness. That's me, and that's Officer Hillman, and that's you, no question. May I have this? I don't want it to fall into enemy hands."

"Sure." I handed it to him.

"Donni, off the record. Just between you and me.

Truth." He looked quizzical. "Weren't you having a little bit of fun with me when you created this?"

"Yeah. I was."

"And the riding-the-school one?"

"It was partly serious. But, yeah, I was mocking you a little."

He smiled and nodded. "I thought so." He held up his new picture and looked at it again. "I am going to have this framed and I will hang it in my home if I can get my wife to agree. It'll remind me."

"Remind you what?"

"To be humble."

I wasn't sure what he meant by that, but I didn't ask.

We talked a little more about what I should paint for his office. He didn't want anything with him in it. Nature scenes, maybe. "Why don't you come into school and work in the art room?" he suggested. "That way I could see how it's going. Mrs. Antonio would love to have you."

"Um," I said.

"No regular schedule," he said. "No regular classes. Just ask one of the secretaries for a visitor's pass. And, Donni"—he was on his way out the door, but he turned—"*when* you feel up to it, and not a minute before, come to my office and just visit."

"I see what you're doing," I said. "You're trying to ease me back in."

"Well, yes. Yes, I am. But I also want some good art for my office. Is that okay?"

"I'll, um, I'll see," I said, but I knew I was going to do it. I couldn't resist. My mind was already making pictures of what to put on his boring, blank tan walls.

"Is Trisha still real mad at me?" I asked Mom while I was dishing up the take-out Chinese she had brought for lunch.

"I don't know. Why don't you call her and see?"

"I did, last night. She hung up on me."

"Then I guess she's still mad."

"I, uh, what I'm really asking—"

"Yes?"

"Never mind." What I was trying to ask was for Mom to get Trisha to forgive me. But I knew that was up to me.

I'd been thinking and thinking about how to make it up to Trisha. Even though I was kind of worrying about myself, what with all the doctors and everything, and I had home schooling and Mr. Billet to think about, I was still thinking about Trisha almost all the time. I kept trying to think what picture I could paint her and give to her that would make her happy. A picture of her and me together? A picture of me offering her a heart on the palm of my hand? A picture of a big, sorry, teary attack heart giving her a hug? Nothing seemed right. The more I thought about it, the more I kept thinking what Mr. Billet had said, that I used art as a crutch. I sort of didn't and I sort of did. Painting a picture for Trisha would be better than nothing, but it would be kind of like hiding behind my art, kind of a coward's way of apologizing. Art was my thing. It wasn't Trisha's thing.

As Mom and I dug into the Szechuan chicken with mushrooms, though, suddenly I knew what I had to do for Trisha.

My fortune cookie said: "Happiness is a butterfly, not a snail."

Right after lunch, right after Mom left, I left, too, and skedaddled down the alley, so she wouldn't see me. I walked as fast as I could to one of the downtown shops, DOS Haus, a computer store. I walked in and looked around until I found a computer that looked like Trisha's. Behind the counter a young round-shouldered guy with a big Adam's apple was watching me with a hint of a sneer, like aren't we the cynic, like he knew I was skipping school, but he didn't care—except I wasn't skipping school, I was excused, but I didn't care what he thought. I asked him, "Can I try out this one?"

"Sure." He came lounging around the counter and turned it on for me. It was pretty much like Trisha's. I started writing. It took awhile because I am not real good at writing, I have to make myself do it, and I hunt the keys when I type. I wrote:

Dear Trisha,

Hi, this is Emmy! You wrote to me a lot and now it's my turn to write to you. Thank you for being a good friend to me and making me come alive and giving me a pretty name. Even though your sister, the hissy-fit expert, erased our files, which she had no right to do, I am still Emmy. I am still your friend and your faithful computer, and I always will be.

I am your friend, so may I tell you something? I am a computer. I know everything, so I know all about Donni, and she is very, very sorry for what she did. You were right about her, she's been upset about the divorce, not to use that as an excuse for her being a selfish jerk, but it might be the reason she had kind of lost sight of the fact that you, Trisha, are a human being. She'd been thinking of you as Trisha the Perfect, so when she read me and found out that you are lonely and have problems the same way she does, well, she zapped straight into ballistic brat mode, like, she's the only one who's allowed? But she knew she was wrong, and right away she felt terrible. She hasn't been able to sleep. She's worried about you and she wants to talk with you.

Trisha, you might think it's funny to get a letter from your computer, but I want you to understand that people do care about you. I care about you, but I'm a computer and I can't give you a hug. Donni can. Ask Donni to give you a hug. She cares about you. Donni loves you very much. And so do I.

Love,
Emmy

My eyes were watery. I looked around and didn't see a printer hooked up to the computer. The round-shouldered guy had his elbows on the counter, watching me with his Elvis sneer.

I asked him, "Can I e-mail this?"

"Like we have the demo computers hooked up to e-mail?" he said real sarcastic.

Oh. I said, "Well, uh, then, can I print it out?"

"This isn't your public media center, kid." He heaved himself up off the counter, came around it, and started toward me, to turn the computer off I guess.

"Please," I said.

"Whatcha writing, a letter to your boyfriend?"

My head started to pound, etc. To heck with all that. I was getting tired of being siiiick—it got in the way of everything. I wanted to keep functioning and talk this guy into printing my letter.

"It's for my sister," I said. My chest hurt, but I took deep breaths to fight the no-air feeling back.

"Sure," he said. "And I'm supposed to print it for you? You going to buy the computer?" He was reaching for the mouse to boot down, but I guess he was curious, he glanced at the screen, and something caught his eye and he started reading. I let him go ahead and read because I didn't know what else to do.

He stood there reading for a couple of minutes. Then he said, "You're Donni, right?"

I nodded.

"Oh, for God's sake," he said, and he turned away and walked off.

Now I didn't know what was going on.

"What kind of printer you want?" he called back real sarcastic.

All of a sudden I felt a lot better. "Just . . . a regular printer. . . ." I wanted the letter to look like it had come off Trisha's computer. Well, as much as possible.

And it did. It looked just like Emmy had printed it out. The computer shop guy brought a printer over and balanced it on top of another computer and plugged it into my computer and checked to make sure there was paper in it and said, "Okay, hit it," like we were pals now. I printed it out and it was perfect.

"Thanks," I said, grabbing the pages from him.

He said, "You know, there's a way of retrieving files from the hard drive even after they've been erased."

"There is?"

"Yeah. If anybody's interested, I can explain it to them."

I thanked him some more and folded the letter carefully and put it deep in the pocket of my bibs, over my heart. And I ran out of there. On my way to see Trisha.

chapter eight

It was after two. By the time I walked six miles out into the country, Trisha would be home from school.

From the DOS Haus I cut down through a development and then I followed a bike trail across fields to a dirt road and then I followed that. I didn't want to walk along the main road because of the yahoos who liked to yell stuff out of truck windows at girls who were walking alone. Even in the middle of town they yelled stuff. So I was walking across country as much as I could. And I was walking as fast as I could.

The whole time I was walking, I was thinking about what might be the best way to give the letter to Trisha. Somehow I didn't think she was going to let me in and take the letter and say thank you and open it up and read it and say oh how nice. She'd rip it up before she ever read it if I didn't have a strategy.

One thing I could do would be to put it in the mail-box. That way Mom would see it and make Trisha read it. I was feeling a lot better about Mom, but I knew better than to think she was perfect. Face it, Mom was nosy. And bossy. Which could be good. I had two good parents. Dad was good for letting a person alone and Mom was good for butting in. Dad was just about perfect for when things were going okay, and Mom was excellent for when there were problems I couldn't fix by myself. All I had to do was learn which was best when.

I could trust Mom to do her stuff. I could put Trisha's letter in the mailbox—

Oops. Trisha would get to the mail first. She always checked the box when she got off the bus.

By the time the dirt road joined up with the main road I still didn't have a plan. I walked along the shoulder of the asphalt, and now every time a car passed me I tensed up, and I couldn't think about anything except walking as fast as I could and what I would do if yahoos noticed me. Maybe stand real still and disguise myself as a fireplug for hound dogs to pee on? I didn't think so. If they wouldn't leave me alone—

A car pulled up beside me. My heart just about stopped. "Young man?"

It was just a gray-haired lady, embarrassed the minute she saw my face. "Uh, Miss, is this Middle Road?"

Yes, she was on the right road. She offered me a ride, but I said no thanks. A minute later, trudging along, I was wondering why I'd done that.

Another car.

Panic time.

Oh, damn, oh double, triple damn, it was Officer Hillman.

He parked his cruiser with the flashers going and got out. "Well, Donni."

I felt cold, hot, sweaty, dizzy, my heart going like a rabbit and all the rest of it but so what. I wasn't going to puke. I had to talk, I had to explain to him. "I'm allowed," I said, which wasn't very clear. I tried to amplify. "I'm not skipping school. Ask Mr. Billet."

"You still shouldn't be out here by yourself," he said. He went back to his car and got on his radio, and I didn't know what was going on. I saw him talking to somebody and nodding for what seemed to be a long time.

Finally he hung it up, got out, and said over the roof of his cruiser to me, "Mr. Billet says to tell you to get a bike."

I nodded. Actually, that was a very good idea. A horse would be even better.

"Where are you going?" Officer Hillman asked.

"My—" He wouldn't know who Trisha was. "My mother's place."

"Get in. I'll drive you. You want to sit in front?"

It was better than sitting in back, I guess. He tried to be nice, telling me what some of the switches on the dashboard were for, but I was glad when we got to the house.

He didn't just drop me off. He parked the cruiser in the driveway and walked to the front door with me, to be sure I'd be safe I guess.

One thing about my old house, when you walk up to the door you can see inside, and because it's way out in the country, Mom doesn't keep the drapes drawn except at night. People just glance in to see if anybody's home.

There on the sofa was Trisha.

Fine, a person's allowed to sit on the sofa. But not Trisha. Trisha was always doing something, she never just sat. But there she was, doing nothing, not even watching TV, curled up on the sofa in a lump, just staring. Everything about her, the way her hands were hanging and her knees were pressed against her chest and her head was drooping, everything said ouch.

Officer Hillman asked, "Who's that?"

"My sister."

"She doesn't look happy."

I didn't say anything. He rang the doorbell, but Trisha didn't even move at first. It was like she didn't have energy to drag her head up. Officer Hillman was reaching for the doorbell again when she slowly lifted her head and looked. Then her eyes widened when she saw a cop standing outside her window and she uncurled and got herself to the door.

"You're not feeling well, Miss?" Officer Hillman asked her as I stepped inside.

"I'm all right." She was her polite Trisha-self for him.

"You sure?"

"I'm fine. Thank you."

"You let me know if there's anything wrong, okay?" He looked at me. "Donni, no more hiking along the road by yourself, right?" He nodded at both of us and went away. Trisha closed the door behind him.

I started to reach for the letter in my pocket. I said, "Trisha—"

"You *scumhead*." She hissed it between her teeth, keeping it low so Officer Hillman wouldn't hear, but from the look on her face she wouldn't have let me into the house if he hadn't happened to be there. "Get out. Go walk in traffic. I hope you get run over. I hope you trip and fall into a pit. Get away from me. Go away and stay away." She was getting louder, Officer Hillman had pulled out of the driveway, and she yanked the door open. "Go on, get out of here!"

Of course I didn't move. So she pushed me. So I tried to shove her hands away. Then she screeched and started whacking at me, whappity, whappity, whappity, with her open hands. She wasn't hurting me, but nobody gets to hit me. I grabbed her wrists hard to make her stop. She struggled, but she couldn't get away from me. She screamed, "I hate you!"

Fine. Great. I hated her, too. Here I was trying to apologize to her and she was hitting me. She made me so mad—

Somebody had to be strong... Donni acts as if she's divorced me... I miss her... I just want to give up...

Trisha pulled loose from me and tried to hit me again. But I put my arms around her and hugged her.

She struggled, she screamed. But the scream turned into a sob. I hugged her and she started crying hard, and I was saying, "I'm sorry, I'm sorry, I'm sorry, I'm sorry, I'm sorry," and patting her back and cuddling her and she bawled and bawled on my shoulder.

After a while her arms went around me and then I wanted to cry.

I didn't because somebody had to be mature, and it was my turn, and about time, huh? When Trisha's crying eased up I said, "C'mon," and I steered her to the sofa and sat her down and handed her the Kleenex, and I went and got a cold wet washcloth from the bathroom and brought it to her. She leaned forward like she felt sick and pressed it to her face, and I sat beside her and waited.

She muttered, "I hate this."

I said, "Trish, I'm really sorry. I'm a twit, I didn't understand."

"Shut up with the sorries."

Good, at least she'd heard me. I shut up.

She crumpled the washcloth in one hand and sat back, laid her head back and closed her eyes. I took the washcloth from her and went and spread it on top of the laundry hamper to dry. When I came back she was still sitting with her eyes closed. I stood in front of her and said, "Listen, Trisha, the guy at the computer store says there's a way to get files back after—"

She opened her eyes and looked at me so red and hard that I shut up. She said, "I don't care about that. I don't want to keep on talking to a stupid computer, damn it. I want a real friend. I want somebody—"

Her voice choked up and she didn't say what kind of somebody, just closed her eyes again. I sat beside her feeling awful.

She said, real shaky, "Everybody likes you better than me."

Oh, come on. Give me a break. "Trish, that's not true. They like you better."

"They do not. Nobody likes me."

What the hell was she talking about? "Trisha, you walk on water! You're the smartest kid in school, you're going to get a scholarship and go to Harvard or something, *and* you're a nice caring person, *and* you're pretty, and you're dependable and responsible and—"

She opened her eyes and glared at me and burst out, "I've got to be that way! If I do one little thing wrong Mom practically disowns me. But you can do just about anything and she's all misty-eyed about how we've got to help you. You throw a fit and she's so full of Donni, Donni, Donni I could be dying and she wouldn't notice!"

I gawked at her, trying to figure out what to do or say. Then I got up and stood in front of her and said, "Hit me."

"Donni—"

"C'mon, hit me." I patted my belly and stuck it out to give her a target. "Make a fist and hit me hard."

"Donni, would you stop being a dork?"

"Hit me."

"I can't, damn it!"

"Well, at least you said damn."

She almost smiled.

"Break something, then. Do something bad right now." I looked around and grabbed one of the throw pillows off the sofa. "Pillow fight!"

"Donni—"

"C'mon, Trisha!" I swung at her lightly.

She looked ticked off, grabbed another pillow and swung back.

I swung just enough to keep her going and on her third swing she clobbered me pretty good, and after that she started to get into it. Pretty soon I didn't have to hold back; it was an even fight. Actually, I hate to admit this, she got me on the run. We fought all over the living room, knocking against furniture and strewing magazines and school papers and wrestling on the floor and banging into the walls. It was great. We split two pillows open and didn't even notice until Trisha saw white fluff snowing all over everything and said, "Uh-oh."

We never decided who won. We just stopped.

"Jeez." Trisha stood up and looked around in a kind of awe. The living room was totally trashed, and we'd never get it cleaned up before Mom came home, and even if we did, we'd have to explain about the pillows.

"Oooooh, Trish, you're in *trouble*," I teased.

"Why me? Why does everything always have to be my fault?"

"You're the *biiig* sister. You're machewer and sponsi-bibble."

"Give me a break!"

"If Mom disowns you," I told her, "come live with Dad and me."

Trisha looked half scared, but then she started to laugh, and it was a good laugh, like she'd really had fun.

We gathered up some of the mess, and then I thought of something. "I have to go to the bathroom." I said, and I did. But while I was upstairs I laid the letter from Emmy on Trisha's pillow, where she would find it when she went to bed.

chapter nine

So a week later I was back in school, sort of, working on Mr. Billet's painting in the art room. It was way better than working at home, because I had an easel and a palette and everything. And people to talk with. I was even glad to see Mrs. Antonio. I had my own brushes and paints, but she gave me all sorts of cool stuff to play with, like opaque watercolors called gouache, and a paint tool, which was sort of a double-ended eraser, and texture sponges. I was messing with the sponges when I heard a quiet voice behind me. "Hi."

"Hey, Trish!" I knew it was her even before I turned around. She stood there with an armload of books nearly up to her chin, smiling a little Mona Lisa smile and studying the paper I was experimenting on.

She asked, "Are those trees?"

"They could be, I guess. Right now they're just sponge monsters." I held up one of the paint sponges.

Her eyes widened. "Mrs. Antonio is letting you use her stuff?"

"Yeah. As long as I don't use it *on* anybody."

"Cool beans." Trish shifted the stack of books in her arms.

I told her, "Put those down, for gosh sake."

She set the books on the table beside my brushes and stuff. Then she looked around for a chair, but there weren't any.

"Sit on the table," I told her.

She kind of leaned against the table, I guess because sitting on tables or desks is against the rules, although the teachers do it all the time. "Are those new jeans?" she asked.

"Yeah." New for me, anyway. Really great, funky, old flare-legged jeans from Goodwill.

"I like them," Trish said.

I eyed her clothes—brown slacks like the office ladies wore, a beige sweater, hair pulled back in those brown clips they call tortoiseshell and on a turtle they might have looked good. I blurted, "Trish, do you like *your* outfit?"

"Huh?" She looked down at herself, then she looked at me. "What's wrong with it?"

"Nothing." Actually, everything. If she wore a sign advertising I'M A NERD she couldn't have done much better. But I didn't want to get into a fight with her. "Never mind." I grabbed the paint tool and started scraping gray bones into the sponge monsters.

Behind me, Trish asked, "Did you get your poetry paper back?"

"Yeah. I got a B." For me, this was fantabulous. I'd done the paper on the poem I liked, "Fern Hill" by Dylan Thomas.

"Rats," Trish said.

I peered at her. "Trish, B is good!"

"The one I ripped up would have gotten an A."

"No, it wouldn't." It probably would have gotten a D. The teacher adored Emily Dickinson.

She said, "B is better than nothing, I guess. Have you decided what you're going to paint for Mr. Billet?"

"Maybe . . . I dunno. He wants some kind of nature scene." I realized that my so-called sponge monsters really did look like trees. Trish was right; the sponge texture made great foliage. Blue and crimson trees, why not? I grabbed for the gouache. White tree trunks. Monster big gray-white-brown-green trunks and branches and touch up the foliage with some green and some shading and—I forgot Trish was there. I jumped when she said, "In answer to your question, no."

"Huh?" I turned to stare at her. Didn't know what she was talking about.

"No, I don't like my outfit. I hate all my clothes."

"Well, make Mom get you something else, then!" I didn't want to talk about clothes. I wanted to paint.

"I can't," Trish said.

"Yes, you can. If she says no, keep asking."

"I can't!"

"Sure, you can! Whine a little for once!"

"Donni, I just can't! I can't bother her."

Something in her face made me put down my paint-brush.

We looked at each other.

"I'm not you," Trish said.

"Well, heck no. Why would you want to be me?"

She actually smiled.

"Dad would get you new clothes," I said.

"That's not the point."

"What is the point, Trish?"

Her smile faded. She just studied me, frowning like I was a calculus problem that was giving her trouble. Or maybe she was looking at me but thinking about something else. "Can't I just be a nerd?" she asked finally.

"Sure, if that's what you want."

She just stood there.

"Well?" I prompted.

"Well, what?"

"Well, is being a nerd what you want?"

"Oh, shut up, Donni." She didn't sound like a nerd. "Give me a break. You are such a pain."

I grinned, picked up my favorite big sable brush and kept on painting. Under the trees I roughed in some deer, then a python and a couple of peacocks and a unicorn. I knew what to paint now. Sunny sky, maybe some blue roses, wild canaries in the pomegranate trees, and coatimundis, swans, ponies, Gila monsters, Galapagos tortoises, possums, cheetahs, griffins, sparrow hawks, meerkats, marmots, lots of animals, all kinds. And far away in the distance, so you could just barely see them, people. A family. A man, a woman, a couple of little kids. I mean, Eden got shot long ago, but I could still paint it, right? I could paint whatever I wanted.